Puppy Friends #4

Lenny the Lazy Puppy

by Jenny Dale

Illustrated by Frank Rodgers

Aladdin Paperbacks

New York   London   Toronto   Sydney   Singapore

Look for these PUPPY FRIENDS books!

#1 *Gus the Greedy Puppy*
#2 *Lily the Lost Puppy*
#3 *Spot the Sporty Puppy*

Coming soon

#5 *Max the Muddy Puppy*

First Aladdin Paperbacks edition May 2000

Text copyright © 1999 by Working Partners Limited
Illustrations copyright © 1999 by Frank Rodgers
Activity Fun Pages text copyright © 2000 by Stasia Ward Kehoe
First published 1999 by Macmillan Children's Books U.K.
Created by Working Partners Limited

Aladdin Paperbacks
An imprint of Simon & Schuster
Children's Publishing Division
1230 Avenue of the Americas
New York, NY 10020

Library of Congress Catalog Card Number: 00-102141
ISBN 0-689-83552-3

Chapter One

"Come on, Lenny! Fetch!" shouted Lauren. "Fetch the ball!" She threw the ball up into the sky in a wide arc, and it bounced down onto the grass.

Lenny, who was lying in the sun, opened one eye and yawned. Then he closed it again.

"I thought he was supposed to be a retriever," said Lauren's best friend, Michelle.

"He is," Lauren replied with a grin.

"Well, that means he's supposed to run after things and bring them back, doesn't it?" Michelle pointed out.

Only when I want to, Lenny thought lazily. He yawned again. It was quite a long walk from the Millers' house to the park and now that they'd arrived, he wanted to have a snooze. He didn't want to run up and down after a silly old ball. Besides, he knew that Lauren would run after it and bring it back anyway if he didn't.

"He's *supposed* to retrieve things, but he doesn't," said Mr. Miller, Lauren's father. They were strolling along a broad path between some beautiful rose bushes. "I don't think I've ever seen a lazier puppy!"

What a wise guy! Lenny thought indignantly. *I'm not lazy. I'm just saving my energy.*

"Come and play keep away, Dad," Lauren called, running back with the ball in her hand.

"Um . . . no thanks, love," said Mr. Miller. "I'll just sit on that bench over there and read my newspaper."

Lenny sat up when he heard that. "And he says *I'm* lazy!" he barked.

Lauren went over and stroked her puppy's shaggy golden coat. "Sure you don't want to play, Lenny?"

Lenny licked her hand. He loved

Lauren, but he really didn't want to run around and get all hot and out of breath. He wanted to snooze in the warm sun.

Lauren and Michelle ran off together across the park and began throwing the ball to each other. They were quite a long way away from Lenny, but he could just about hear what they were saying.

"I had a great time at your birthday

party yesterday," Michelle called to Lauren.

So did I, Lenny thought dreamily. He had sat under the table all afternoon, waiting for bits of birthday food to be dropped near him.

"I loved the present you bought me," Lauren called back.

Lenny opened one eye and woofed his agreement. Michelle had given Lauren a pencil case with pictures of puppies just like Lenny all over it.

"Have you decided what you're going to buy with the birthday money your gran and aunt sent you?" Michelle asked.

Lauren shook her head. "Not yet."

Lenny stopped listening to the two girls and began to doze off. The sun felt deliciously warm on his furry coat, and the long grass underneath him was soft and springy. He stretched out his shaggy paws and settled down even more comfortably.

"Dad!" Just as he was drifting off to sleep, Lenny heard Lauren calling her father. "Dad! We've lost the ball in the bushes and we can't find it!"

Mr. Miller looked over the top of his newspaper. "Have you had a *good* look?" he asked.

"Yes, we have," Lauren told him. "But we can't see it anywhere."

"We could get Lenny to help us look for it," Michelle suggested.

"We'll be here all day if we do that!" Mr. Miller answered, smiling. He folded his newspaper and stood up. "Come on, I'll give you a hand."

Good, Lenny thought happily. *Now I can have a nice snooze in peace and quiet.*

A few seconds later, he was fast asleep, dreaming of big, juicy bones. . . .

"Dad! Dad!"

Lenny woke up suddenly. Lauren was calling again. He didn't know how long he'd been asleep, but it could only have been a few minutes. He looked up to see Lauren and Michelle, looking very upset, standing on the grass where they had been playing ball.

Lenny jumped to his feet and dashed over to the two girls. He couldn't bear it when Lauren was unhappy.

Mr. Miller came out of the bushes. He had bits of leaves and twigs in his hair, but he was clutching the ball triumphantly. "What's the matter, Lauren?"

"My—my jacket!" Lauren said tearfully. "I left it here on the grass while we were playing, and now it's gone!"

"Oh, Lauren, what did you go and do a silly thing like that for?" Her father sighed and shook his head. "Someone must have taken it while we were looking for the ball."

Lenny whined and pawed at Lauren's leg. He wished now that he hadn't gone to sleep. Maybe then he would have seen what had happened to her jacket.

"What did you have in the pockets?" Mr. Miller went on. "Anything important?"

Now Lauren began to cry. "My birthday money!" she sobbed. "All my birthday money was in it!"

"Oh, *Lauren!*" said her father again, looking cross. "You should have given it to me to look after."

"Don't worry, Lauren," Michelle said. She put an arm around her friend's shoulder. "Come on, we'll have a look around and see if we can find it."

Lenny felt very bad indeed. If he'd stayed awake and guarded Lauren's jacket, then it wouldn't have been taken. He slumped at Lauren's feet. "It's all my fault," he snuffled to himself.

Then Lenny sat up again. "I have to try to make things right," he told himself sternly. He licked Lauren's knee. "Don't worry, Lauren," he woofed. "I'm going to find your jacket."

Lauren bent down and ruffled Lenny's ear, but she and Michelle and Mr. Miller were busy deciding where to search for the jacket. They didn't see Lenny carefully sniffing the grass, then hurrying away, his nose glued to the ground.

Lenny wasn't worried about going off on his own. He knew how to find his way back home from the park if he had to. The most important thing now was to find Lauren's jacket—and get her birthday money back.

He was a retriever, wasn't he? Well, now he was going to retrieve that missing jacket!

Chapter Two

At first Lenny was confused—there were so many smells around. But his sharp nose soon picked up Lauren's scent. As he began to follow the trail, Lenny detected the scents of two other people as well. *They must be the ones who took the jacket,* he thought indignantly.

Sniffing this way and that, Lenny

followed the trail off the grass and onto the path. He went along quite slowly. There were so many smells that it was sometimes hard to pick out the one he was looking for. He trotted farther and farther down the winding path.

"It's not here!" Lauren said, beginning to cry again. She, Michelle, and Mr. Miller had searched every inch of the grass where they had been playing, and they'd even looked in the bushes. But there was no sign of her jacket.

"Someone might have picked it up and taken it to the park ranger's office," Michelle suggested.

Mr. Miller nodded. "That's a good

idea," he said. "I'm sure the park ranger looks after lost property. We'd better go and try there."

"Where's Lenny?" Lauren asked suddenly, looking around. "Lenny! Lenny! Come here, boy!" But there was no sign of her retriever puppy.

"Oh, no!" Lauren cried. "Now we've lost Lenny, too!"

"He's probably asleep somewhere," Mr. Miller said crossly. "We'll just have to keep calling him until he wakes up."

"Maybe he's gone to look for your jacket!" Michelle suggested brightly. "He is a *retriever*, after all!"

Mr. Miller shook his head and smiled. "I don't think so," he replied. "That puppy couldn't retrieve a bone if it was put right under his nose!" He picked up his newspaper from the bench. "Come on, you two. Let's go and find the park ranger—we can look for Lenny on the way."

Lenny was concentrating so hard that he didn't hear the footsteps behind him. Then someone spoke.

"I don't like stray dogs running around my park, Danny," said a stern voice. "If you find one, just call the dog pound—they'll come and take it. Understand? There are far too many strays around here."

Lenny stopped in his tracks. He knew that voice! It was Mr. Fraser, the park ranger. All the dogs who came to the park were scared of Mr. Fraser. He was a tall, fierce-looking man with a little mustache, and he patrolled the park with an eagle eye. He didn't like litter, he didn't like noisy children, and he didn't like dogs—especially stray dogs.

Lenny wasn't a stray, and the tag on his collar had his name and his address on it, but he didn't want to take any chances. He dived into a thick clump of bushes and ducked down out of sight.

Mr. Fraser marched down the path, still talking. He was with someone Lenny hadn't seen before—a bored-looking young man with glasses and dark brown hair.

"There's a lot to learn about being an assistant park ranger, Danny," Mr. Fraser was saying. "This is only your first day on the job, so make sure you keep your eyes and ears open."

"Yeah, okay," said Danny with a yawn.

"Yes, *Mr. Fraser*, if you don't mind," snapped Mr. Fraser, frowning.

Lenny waited until the two men had gone by. Then he tried to jump out of the bushes. But he couldn't move—his collar had gotten caught on a large twig!

Lenny struggled and strained, frantically trying to free himself. But it was no use—he was totally stuck. There was only one thing left to do. Pulling backward really hard, he squeezed his head out of the collar, leaving it hanging on the bush.

He was free! But now that he didn't have a collar and tag on, he'd have to keep a sharp lookout for the two park rangers.

Lenny hurried over to the path again and sniffed around until he picked up

the trail. After a few minutes it led him toward the large lake in the middle of the park. Then, suddenly, the trail stopped.

Lenny's heart sank. He ran around frantically in circles trying to pick up the scent again, but it was no good. There were just too many mixed-up smells for him to find the one he was looking for.

He wandered along the water's edge, sniffing the ground. There were lots of ducks on the lake, as well as two swans, which bobbed up and down in the water hunting for leftover bits of bread. Lenny kept a wary eye on them. He'd chased the swans once before when he'd come to the park. One of them had given him a nasty nip with its strong beak. Lenny hadn't chased the swans since!

Lenny stopped sniffing and began to feel miserable. It looked as if he would have to go back to Lauren without finding her jacket after all. Some retriever he had turned out to be. He hadn't really found *anything*.

Lenny yawned and lay down under a

tree. He was feeling a little tired. All that running around had worn him out. Maybe he'd just have a little rest before he started looking again. . . .

"Hey, you!" shouted a loud, familiar voice, which made Lenny quiver all over with fear. "Get away from the water and stop chasing those ducks!"

It was Mr. Fraser, the park ranger!

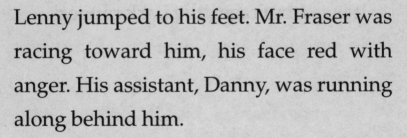

Chapter Three

Lenny jumped to his feet. Mr. Fraser was racing toward him, his face red with anger. His assistant, Danny, was running along behind him.

Lenny couldn't risk getting caught now that he didn't have his collar on! He turned and ran for his life. He raced away from the water's edge and back up the path. Mr. Fraser and

Danny were in hot pursuit.

"Come on, Danny, can't you run any faster?" grumbled Mr. Fraser as he rumbled along. "I want that dog caught—it's got no collar on—obviously a stray!"

"I'm — doing — my — best!" Danny wheezed, panting heavily.

"A young lad like you should be able to run faster than that!" Mr. Fraser told him sternly. "*Aargh!* Get out of my way, you stupid creatures!"

The park ranger had to skid to a sudden halt as a crowd of ducks, and the two swans, waddled eagerly toward them, hoping to be fed.

Danny wasn't expecting Mr. Fraser to stop quite so suddenly, and he crashed into the back of the park ranger, almost sending Mr. Fraser into the lake head-first.

"Why don't you look where you're going!" roared Mr. Fraser.

"It wasn't my fault!" Danny said

indignantly. "You shouldn't have stopped like that!"

Mr. Fraser glared at his new assistant. "I want that dog caught before it causes any damage in my park!" he bellowed. "Ow!" Mr. Fraser jumped back as an angry swan nipped smartly at his ankle.

Lenny didn't stop running until he was a long way from the lake. Then he turned around and looked behind him. Mr. Fraser and Danny were nowhere to be seen, thank goodness.

Lenny didn't know what to do. He was tired out and he'd lost the trail of Lauren's jacket. He'd never find it now.

He padded slowly down the path and

back toward the place where Lauren and Michelle had been playing ball. He was looking forward to having his usual afternoon nap when they got home, but he really wished he'd been able to find Lauren's jacket.

While Lenny was busy running away from the park rangers, Lauren, Michelle, and Mr. Miller had made their way to the office. It was a small, square, wooden building which looked a lot like a shed. It stood on the other side of the park, near the tennis courts.

"I hope someone's handed the jacket in," Mr. Miller said as they walked along the path.

"So do I," Michelle added.

But Lauren wasn't listening. She was looking around the park and frowning. "I'm more worried about Lenny," she said. "This is a big park—what if he really is lost?"

"Oh, I'm sure he's around here some-where," Mr. Miller replied as they stopped outside the office. "He's too lazy to have gone far. He'll come back if we shout loud enough."

"I don't think the park ranger's here," said Michelle.

Mr. Miller knocked on the door, but no one answered. Then he tried the han-dle, but the door was locked. Mr. Miller looked through the window. There was

no sign of Lauren's jacket inside the small office.

"What are we going to do now?" Michelle asked, looking worried.

"I want to go and find Lenny," Lauren said firmly. "He might be getting scared, being all alone."

Mr. Miller smiled. "I imagine he's asleep somewhere, safe and sound."

"I don't care," Lauren said stubbornly. "I don't care about my jacket or my birthday money, as long as I get Lenny back!"

"Come on, then," said Mr. Miller with a sigh. "We'd better go and look for him. . . . "

Lenny arrived back at the place where Lauren's jacket had gone missing. He was feeling so tired, he could hardly put one paw in front of the other. He couldn't wait to get home. But there was no sign of Lauren, Michelle, or Mr. Miller. Lenny wondered where they were. He was sure Lauren wouldn't have gone home without him. They must be somewhere in the park.

He sniffed around until he picked up

their trail and, with his nose to the ground, began to follow it.

The scent led him back to the path, then in the opposite direction, away from the lake. Lenny was glad. He didn't want to meet Mr. Fraser and Danny again!

Lenny trotted on for a while, concentrating hard. But suddenly he picked up another scent. He stopped, feeling very excited. "That's the two people I followed before!" Lenny snuffled to himself. And the scent was getting stronger and stronger. . . .

Lenny raised his head and saw two boys coming down the path toward him. They were arguing at the tops of their voices and one of them was carrying

something over his arm. Lenny recognized it right away. It was Lauren's
jacket!

Chapter Four

Lenny stared angrily at the two boys as they came nearer. Had they *stolen* Lauren's jacket?

Lenny began to growl softly, deep in his throat. If they had stolen it, they were in for a surprise!

"I thought you said you knew where the park ranger's office is, Jamie!" the smallest of the two boys grumbled as they came closer. "We've been walking around for ages now—Mom's going to be mad at us for being late!"

"Well, we can't just leave the jacket here, can we, Ben?" said Jamie. "Someone might be looking for it."

Lenny stopped growling. It sounded as if they two boys had found Lauren's jacket lying on the grass and decided to hand it in at the office, but they must have lost their way.

"Let's take it home with us," suggested Ben. "Mom will know what to do."

Lenny whimpered softly. If the two boys took the jacket home with them, Lauren might *never* get it back! There was only one thing to do. He padded down the path to meet the two boys.

"Look, Jamie." Ben nudged his brother. "See that puppy?"

"He looks a bit young to be out on his own, doesn't he?" Jamie kneeled down and held out his hand to Lenny. "Good boy! Come here!"

Lenny rushed over to him. But instead of letting Jamie stroke him, he grabbed the sleeve of Lauren's jacket in his teeth and pulled hard.

"Hey, what are you doing?" Jamie laughed. He tried to tug the sleeve gently out of Lenny's mouth, but the puppy wouldn't let go.

"Maybe he knows who it belongs to," Ben suggested with a grin.

"Don't be silly!" Jamie tugged at the jacket again, but Lenny clung on. "Come and help me get it off him."

Lenny began to feel nervous. He wasn't sure if he could hold onto the coat with two boys pulling at him. He did the only thing he could think of: he growled fiercely.

"Did you hear that?" Ben stopped and

looked at Jamie. "He's dangerous!"

"He's just playing," Jamie replied, but he looked a bit scared himself.

"Well, his tail's not wagging!" Ben pointed out.

Lenny growled again, as fiercely as he could. This time, Jamie dropped the jacket on the ground and backed away, closely followed by his brother.

"All right, all right, we're going!" he told Lenny. "You can *have* the jacket!"

The two boys ran off. Lenny barked happily. He'd done it! He'd gotten the jacket back. Now he was a real retriever!

Lenny was so proud of himself, he felt he might burst! He couldn't wait to hear what Lauren, Michelle, and Mr. Miller would say—*especially* Mr. Miller. They wouldn't be able to call him lazy anymore!

Lenny pushed his nose into the pocket of the jacket. Lauren's wallet was still inside, thank goodness! He tried to lift the jacket off the ground, but it was too heavy.

He'd have to drag it along, he decided. The jacket would get a little dirty, but Lenny didn't think Lauren would mind. After all, she was going to get her birthday money back—thanks to him!

Dragging the jacket was such hard work, Lenny didn't notice two tall shadows creeping through the trees toward him. It wasn't until the very last second that he saw one of the shadows coming up behind him, and by then it was too late. . . .

A hand shot out and firmly grabbed the scruff of Lenny's neck. Lenny howled and tried to wriggle free, but he couldn't.

"Got him!"

"Well done, Danny!" said Mr. Fraser, hurrying to join the assistant park ranger. "Now don't let go!"

"I won't," Danny said importantly. "What do we do now, Mr. Fraser?"

The park ranger frowned at Lenny. "He's not wearing a collar and identity tag, so he must be a stray. We'll have to send him to the dog pound."

Lenny cowered behind Danny's legs.

He felt very frightened. "I don't want to go to the dog pound," he whimpered. "I've got a good home—with Lauren!"

"All right!" said Mr. Fraser. "Let's go back to the office, and we'll phone the dog pound and ask them to come and collect him."

Lenny began to shake with fear. Everything had gone wrong, and now he was in big trouble. If he was take to the dog pound, he might never see Lauren again!

Chapter Five

Lenny looked up at Danny and whined unhappily.

Danny took no notice. "I wonder where that came from?" he said, pointing at Lauren's jacket.

Mr. Fraser picked it up. "Someone must have lost it," he said. "We'll take it back to the office, and it can go into the lost-and-found."

Lenny watched Mr. Fraser reach over to pick up the jacket. The puppy had been *so close* to retrieving Lauren's birthday money—and now she would never know. It just wasn't fair! Lenny was so angry, he couldn't help giving a little growl.

Mr. Fraser dropped the jacket and leaped backward as if he'd been stung by a bee. "That dog growled at me!" he said, glaring at Lenny.

Danny shrugged. "I didn't hear anything."

Mr. Fraser stared hard at Lenny and shook his head. "You can pick up the jacket, Danny," he muttered.

"What?" Danny said. "I thought I was

supposed to be holding the dog!"

"Well, you can pick up the jacket, too, can't you?" Mr. Fraser snapped.

Danny looked annoyed. "Okay, you hold the dog and I'll get the jacket." Danny began to drag Lenny closer to the park ranger.

"Uh . . . no!" cried Mr. Fraser, backing away. "No, you keep hold of him," he said.

Lenny noticed that the park ranger didn't look at all scary now. In fact, he looked *scared!* In a flash, Lenny realized something very interesting . . . Mr. Fraser was frightened of him!

"Look, make up your mind, Mr. Fraser," Danny said rudely. "Do you want me to get the jacket, or do you want me to hold the dog?"

Before the park ranger could reply, Lenny tried another growl—a big, deep, fierce one this time.

Mr. Fraser turned even paler, and this time Danny looked a bit nervous, too.

"He's starting to get angry," Danny said, looking worried. "What shall I do?"

"You're not frightened of a young pup like that, are you?" said Mr. Fraser in a shaky voice. The park ranger was pretending not to be scared, but Lenny knew better.

Lenny decided to help things along by growling loudly again and pretending to nip Danny's leg. Danny gave a howl of alarm and let go of Lenny.

Gleefully, Lenny rushed toward the terrified Mr. Fraser.

"You idiot, Danny!" Mr. Fraser roared. "He'll attack me now!"

The park ranger tried to run, but he tripped and fell over. "*Aargh!*" he cried as the puppy bounded toward him.

At the last second, Lenny swerved past the quivering Mr. Fraser and pounced on Lauren's jacket. He wasn't going to let them take it—and he wasn't going to let them send him to the dog pound.

"Do something, Danny!" shouted Mr. Fraser, who had now leaped up and taken cover behind a nearby tree.

Danny hesitated. Then he slipped off his coat and, holding it out in front of him, started to walk slowly toward Lenny.

"Come on, boy," he said softly. "Good dog. Now keep still, you stupid mutt...."

Lenny growled, but Danny kept on coming toward him. Lenny knew that the man was going to grab him, but how could he run away? He had to stay and guard Lauren's jacket! Lenny braced himself. . . .

Chapter Six

"What on earth's going on here?"

With a whimper of relief, Lenny recognized Mr. Miller's deep voice.

Danny stopped in his tracks.

"Lenny!"

Lenny knew that voice, too. It was the one he loved most in the whole world—Lauren's!

He turned around and barked joyfully. There were Lauren and Mr. Miller and Michelle. Thank goodness!

Lauren dashed down the path and scooped her puppy into her arms. Lenny wriggled happily, trying to lick Lauren's face while she kissed the top of his head.

Mr. Miller looked at Danny, who was still holding out his coat, ready to trap Lenny. Then he looked over at Mr. Fraser, who was still behind the tree. "What's up? Is everything all right?" he asked.

Before anyone could answer, Lauren spotted her jacket lying on the ground. "There it is!" she gasped.

"So this jacket's yours then, miss?" Danny asked her. Lauren nodded. "And the dog, too?"

Lauren nodded again and hugged Lenny closer.

"We thought he was a stray," Mr. Fraser said, coming out from behind the tree. "Why hasn't he got a collar on?"

"He *did* have one," Lauren replied, looking at Lenny's neck. "He must have lost it."

Lenny licked Lauren's chin to show he agreed.

"You see, I lost my jacket," Lauren explained. "And while we were looking for it, Lenny went missing, too. Then I didn't care about the jacket—I just wanted my puppy back."

Lenny's heart swelled with love. Lauren cared about him as much as he cared about her.

"The pup had the jacket when we caught him," Mr. Fraser explained. "We don't know where he got it from."

"Hang on a minute," said Mr. Miller,

looking surprised. "Are you telling us that *Lenny* found this jacket?"

Mr. Fraser and Danny looked at each other, then nodded.

"Lenny!" cried Lauren delightedly. "You clever boy! I *knew* you could do it!"

Lenny's tail wagged madly.

"You're a hero, Lenny!" said Michelle, scratching the puppy's ears.

Lenny woofed his thanks.

Mr. Miller smiled. "I thought you were far too lazy to be a good retriever, Lenny. But I take it all back! Well done!"

Lenny barked and wagged his tail again. He could get used to all this praise!

"We were going to take the jacket to our office, weren't we, Mr. Fraser?"

Danny said with a grin. "But the puppy didn't want us to. And then when he started growling, Mr. Fraser got scared—"

"That's enough, thank you, Danny," said Mr. Fraser hurriedly.

"Oh, but Lenny's really friendly!" Lauren said, carrying the puppy up to the park ranger. "Look, you can pet him if you like!"

Mr. Fraser looked as if he'd rather pet a man-eating tiger, but he put out a cautious hand and touched the top of the puppy's head.

Lenny gave a little woof, and Mr. Fraser jumped back, looking alarmed.

"He's just saying hello!" Lauren grinned.

Mr. Fraser smiled weakly and gave

Lenny another little pat.

Lenny wagged his tail like crazy. He couldn't *wait* to tell the other dogs he met in the park that he'd just made friends with the fearsome Mr. Fraser!

"I think we'd better go home," Mr. Miller said with a grin as Lenny yawned widely. "I think Lenny needs a nap—all that excitement must have tired him out!"

"It has!" Lenny woofed, yawning again.

"I'll carry you home, boy," said Lauren.

They said goodbye to Danny and Mr. Fraser and set off for home.

Lenny snuggled down happily in Lauren's arms. He was going to enjoy coming to the park much more now that he wasn't scared of Mr. Fraser.

"See, Dad?" said Lauren as they walked toward the park gates. "Lenny *did* find my jacket!"

"Yes, Lenny did very well," Mr. Miller replied. "I thought he was too lazy to be a proper retriever, but he proved me wrong."

"Yes, I did," Lenny woofed proudly . . . and then he fell asleep.

Puppy Friends Activity Fun Pages

Developed by Stasia Ward Kehoe

Lazy Lenny Trivia Quiz

1. What breed of dog is Lenny?
2. Who is Lauren's best friend?
3. What kinds of pictures are on Lauren's new pencil case?
4. What is in the pocket of Lauren's lost jacket?
5. What is the name of the new assistant park ranger?

(see answers at bottom of page)

Plan Your Own Park

The park in which Lauren loses her jacket sounds like a lovely place. It has trails, bushes, and a lake with swans. If you could design your own park, what would it contain? Would there be nature trails, special trees or flowers, swings, a lake or pond, a fountain, a sandbox, or other fun features? On a large sheet of paper, draw your plans for the perfect park. Make sure to include lots of interesting details, like the

Answers: 1. A retriever 2. Michelle 3. Puppies 4. Birthday money 5. Danny names of the trees and flowers, or the kinds of animals and birds that would live in your park. Think of a special name for your park and write it at the top of the paper.

A Puppy's Point of View

Readers follow parts of the search for Lauren's lost jacket from Lenny's point of view. We learn how Lenny is anxious, confused, determined, and even sleepy. Try writing your own short story from a puppy's point of view. The story could be about a dog searching for a lost toy or a snack, a dog being chased by dog catchers, a dog getting ready for a nap, or a topic of your choice. Draw pictures of your dog's different facial expressions, depending on how he is feeling, in order to illustrate your story.

Puppy Lullaby

At the end of the story, Lenny is one tired pup. Make up your own lullaby with soothing words just right for a dog like Lenny. Set your words to a sleepy tune like "Rock-a-bye Baby" or "Lullaby and

Goodnight." Sing the new puppy lullaby to your favorite canine companion.

Delightful Dog Charm

To make a sweet medallion for yourself or a puppy-loving pal, you will need:

Three pipe cleaners, ideally in assorted colors

A small photograph, drawing, or magazine picture of a dog

A small piece of light cardboard (such as one side of an empty cereal box)

Safety scissors

Craft glue

A length of colored yarn or string (about 30")

Carefully trim your dog picture into a square, circle, or triangle shape, making sure to leave a little space around the dog. Lay the trimmed picture on the cardboard. Trace, then cut, the shape out of the cardboard. Glue the picture onto the cardboard. Twist or braid the pipe cleaners together. Keeping the ends together at the top center, bend the pipe cleaner braid to fit the edge of your picture like a frame. Twist the ends into a hanging loop. Dab the edges of the picture with glue, then press the pipe cleaner frame on firmly.

Place a book or other heavy object on top of the picture and frame to hold in place until the glue dries. Thread the colored string through the top pipe cleaner loop and tie the ends to make a necklace for your delightful dog charm.

Puppy Care Pointer: Keeping Clean

Puppies do not need a great deal of grooming. A daily brushing with a soft brush is probably a good plan. To remove lots of dirt or mud, use a damp cloth. Some experts do not recommend complete baths for puppies during their first year because soap can remove a pup's natural protective skin oils. Check with your veterinarian to be certain you are properly cleaning your dog. And after bathing a dog, always be sure to keep him inside until he's completely dry, especially when the weather is cold.

Everyone needs Kitten Friends!

Fluffy and fun, purry and huggable, what could be more perfect than a kitten?

by

Jenny Dale

#1 Felix the Fluffy Kitten
0-689-84108-6 $3.99

#2 Bob the Bouncy Kitten
0-689-84109-4 $3.99

#3 Star the Snowy Kitten
0-689-84110-8 $3.99

#4 Nell the Naughty Kitten
0-689-84029-2 $3.99

#5 Leo the Lucky Kitten
0-689-84030-6 $3.99

#6 Patch the Perfect Kitten
0-689-84031-4 $3.99